All Kinds of Kisses

For Graham —H. S.

A FEIWEL AND FRIENDS BOOK
An Imprint of Macmillan
ALL KINDS OF KISSES. Text copyright © 2016 by Heather Swain. Illustrations copyright © 2016 by Steven Henry.
All rights reserved. Printed in China by RR Donnelley Asia Printing Solutions Ltd., Dongguan City,
Guangdong Province. For information, address Feiwel and Friends, 175 Fifth Avenue, New York, N.Y. 10010.

Our books may be purchased in bulk for promotional, educational, or business use. Please contact your local
bookseller or the Macmillan Corporate and Premium Sales Department at (800) 221-7945 ext. 5442 or
by e-mail at MacmillanSpecialMarkets@macmillan.com.

Library of Congress Cataloging-in-Publication Data
Names: Swain, Heather, 1969– author. | Henry, Steven, 1962– illustrator.
Title: All kinds of kisses / Heather Swain ; illustrated by Steven Henry.
Description: First Edition. | New York : Feiwel & Friends, 2016. | Summary: "A celebration of the ways in which
animals kiss their babies"—Provided by publisher.
Identifiers: LCCN 2015036477 | ISBN 9781250066503 (hardback)
Subjects: | CYAC: Kissing—Fiction. | Animals—Fiction. | BISAC: JUVENILE FICTION /
Animals / General. | JUVENILE FICTION / Family / New Baby.
Classification: LCC PZ7.S9698934 Al 2016 | DDC [E]—dc23
LC record available at http://lccn.loc.gov/2015036477

Book design by Eileen Savage
Feiwel and Friends logo designed by Filomena Tuosto

First Edition—2016
The illustrations for this book began as pencil drawings on Bienfang marker paper, which
were then scanned and painted digitally in Corel Painter 2015 using modified Impasto brushes.

1 3 5 7 9 10 8 6 4 2

mackids.com

All Kinds of Kisses

Heather Swain

Illustrated by **Steven Henry**

Feiwel and Friends
New York

Humpback whales have gigantic mouths to gobble up great gulps of shrimp.

And through all the bubbles, mamas give cuddles and big, wet canoodles to calves.

How would a humpback whale kiss?

Daddy sun bear has a lovely long
tongue for lapping up honey
from hives.

"You're so scrumptious and
yummy, I'll nuzzle your tummy."
 "Yippee!" the baby replies.

How would a sun bear kiss?

Red crossbill birds have twisted beaks to tweeze tiny seeds out of cones.

"That way or this?" asks granny crossbill while pecking a quick, crooked kiss.

How would a crossbill kiss?

The piranha's maw has a fine jutting
jaw for nibbling on fish fins and fruit.

"I'm coming in for a peck on the chin," says papa piranha. "You're cute!"

How would a piranha kiss?

Several quick flicks of mama
anteater's tongue will clean
out a mound of termites.

"After a snack, hop on my back
for a quick kiss and then it's good
night."

How would an anteater kiss?

A grasshopper mouth opens east-west,
but not north-south. They're like scissors
for chopping up leaves.

"Don't try to hide from a kiss on its
side," says grandpa grasshopper to
nymphs.

How would a grasshopper kiss?

The flexible lips of a giraffe twist to pull leaves off very tall trees.

"Please don't be fickle over a little lip tickle," says grandma giraffe to her calf, who giggles and wiggles his knees.

How would a giraffe kiss?

The sweet little tree frog has no lips
for a snog, but her tongue shoots out
like a spring.

"Stand back," says her mother,
"'cause one way or another, I'm getting
a smooch with this thing."

How would a tree frog kiss?

What a cute little mouth a pink
porpoise has, just perfect for
plucking out fish.

"Pucker up," says aunt porpoise
as she swims by the babe,
in search of a fine, dainty kiss.

How would a porpoise kiss?

With tongues shaped like straws for slurping sweet nectar, hummingbird chicks are in for a treat.

While flitting through flowers for
hours and hours,
mama kisses them lickety-split.

How would a hummingbird kiss?

A creek chubsucker has soft, flabby lips to vacuum the riverbed.

"Mmmm-wah, mmm-wah!" says uncle chubsucker, who gives a big pucker and plants one on baby's head.

How would a sucker fish kiss?

Duck-billed platypus has a flat snout for digging up yabbies and grubs.

"Come here, little puggles, it's time for snuggles," says papa platypus, giving out hugs.

How would a platypus kiss?

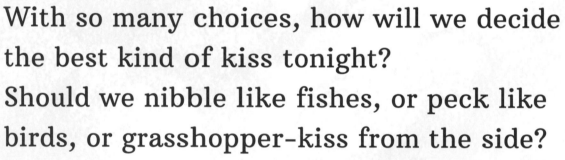

With so many choices, how will we decide
the best kind of kiss tonight?
Should we nibble like fishes, or peck like
birds, or grasshopper-kiss from the side?

Whichever it is, this much is true:
when we say good night,
I love all kinds of kisses from you!

Fun Facts

The mouth of a **humpback whale** is about one-third the size of its body. Babies spend almost a year nursing and swimming near their mamas.

Although **sun bears** are the smallest kind of bears, they have comically long tongues for getting honey from beehives, insects from trees, and termites from mounds. Sun bear cubs hum while nursing and cry when they need attention from their mothers.

Crossbills use their crisscross beaks to pry the scales off pinecones to get at the hidden seeds inside. Since they feed the seeds to their chicks, they can breed anytime they find enough food.

Piranhas are freshwater fish that use their powerful teeth to eat both animals (like snails and fish) and plants (like seeds and fruit that fall into the water). Mother piranhas can lay up to 5,000 eggs, which are cared for by both males and females, so most of them survive until hatching.

Anteaters have very long snouts and powerful tongues but no teeth. They can slurp up to 35,000 ants and termites every day by flicking their tongues about 160 times per minute while feeding. A baby can hitch rides on its mother's back for the first year of life, but then it has to walk.

Unlike our mouths, a **grasshopper's** mouth is turned sideways and has two sharp, jagged jaws that work like scissors to cut up all kinds of plants. Grasshopper mothers lay eggs in pods underground that hatch ten months later. Baby grasshoppers, called nymphs, look like miniature adults.

A **giraffe's** very long neck, flexible lips, and acrobatic tongue help it reach leaves, flowers, and fruit on tall trees.

Mother giraffes stand up when giving birth, so newborns fall nearly six feet to the ground, but they are up and running within an hour!

A tiny **green tree frog** has a long, sticky tongue that's attached at the front of the mouth and curls backward so it can catapult out, snatch up an insect, and get back inside the mouth all in less than a second. Babies hatch from eggs as tadpoles and transform into frogs in about eight weeks.

Pink porpoises (river dolphins that live in the Amazon) are born gray, then become pinker as they age. Their long snouts have lots of powerful teeth inside and tiny hairs outside to help them find and catch fish and crabs. They live in small family groups of up to five to eight dolphins, with babies staying near their mothers for two to three years.

A **hummingbird's** tongue has two tubes that open when they reach nectar. These tubes zip closed as the bird pulls its tongue back into its beak, trapping the nectar to be swallowed. Mother hummingbirds usually have two chicks at a time, and she feeds them by squirting nectar or dropping tiny insects into their beaks.

Creek chubsucker fish have soft, squishy, downward-facing lips that they use to suck up little worms, plants, and tiny crustaceans from the sand and rocks on riverbeds. Females produce about 9,000 eggs per year. Once they hatch, the babies form schools, then swim off alone when they grow up.

Duck-billed platypuses live only in Australia and look like a cross between a duck, an otter, and a beaver. The bill is actually a muzzle covered in leathery skin that can detect the electrical currents of snails, frogs, worms, and little crayfish called yabbies. Unlike other mammals, platypuses lay eggs, then secrete milk that gets lapped up by the babies, which are sometimes called puggles.